Come to the Fairies' Ball

Jane Yolen

Illustrated by

Gary Lippincott

WORDSONG

HONESDALE, PENNSYLVANIA

Text copyright © 2009 by Jane Yolen

Illustrations copyright © 2009 by Gary Lippincott

All rights reserved

Wordsong

An Imprint of Boyds Mills Press, Inc.

815 Church Street

Honesdale, Pennsylvania 18431

Printed in China

CIP data is available.

First edition

The text of this book is set in 24-point Alexa.

The illustrations are done in watercolor.

10 9 8 7 6 5 4 3 2 1

For my fairy twin granddaughters,
Amelia and Caroline
—J.Y.

To my children, your children, and the child in all of us
—G.L.

Come one & come all.
come great & come small.
come winged & come wingless.
bejeweled or ringless.
come
walking or riding.
come
gawking or gliding.
come
soaring or sliding.
Come all, come all
to the
Fairies' Ball.

*I*nvitations delivered in hovel and hall,
In barnyard and arbor,
In treetop and stall.

They all read the same . . .

And then what a tizzy, a flap, and a pother,
A terrible fooforaw, swivet,
and bother,

A twitter, a dither, oh my! what a rumble,
A fret and a fuss and a fidget and grumble.

"Where are my boots?"
   "And where is my crown?"
   "And please tell me,
   Where is my spider-web gown?"
   "Where is my top hat?"
   "And where is my lace?"
   "We've looked everywhere and they're not anyplace!"

"Have you looked in the closet
And under the cot?"

"We've looked and that's where
They're decidedly not."

"Have you looked in the wardrobe
Or next to the stair?"

"We've looked and we've looked
And our garb is not there."

"Have you looked in the bird's nest
Or under the tree?"

"That's not where our best garb
Is likely to be."

"Oh!"

But there was one fairy
Whose dress was too torn
From hanging a year
On a prickly rose thorn.
"Oh dear."

Then dressed in their finest,
In cape, crown, and shawl,
The others all went
To the Fairies' own Ball.
"We're not going to be late!"

They rode off in wagons,
On turtles, on hares.
They were packed piggybacked
Into butterfly chairs.

They were towed there by swans,
They were rowed there by fish,
And one group of five
Got there fast on a wish.

And those who had wings
Flew themselves to the Hall,
And they all came on time
To the Fairies' own Ball.

Except that one fairy,
  Bereft and forlorn,
Whose raggedy dress
  Hung high on the thorn.

She settled herself
On a toadstool and wept
While round and about her
The busy ants crept.

"Do not weep, little fairy,
But do as we do.
Work makes matters better.
You'll see this is true."

"Thank you, ants."

She got up and sewed
    Three petals together
    And used what was left
    For the softest shoe leather.

She fastened the fringe
    Of a fern for a shawl,
    And late—oh so late—
    She took off for the Ball.

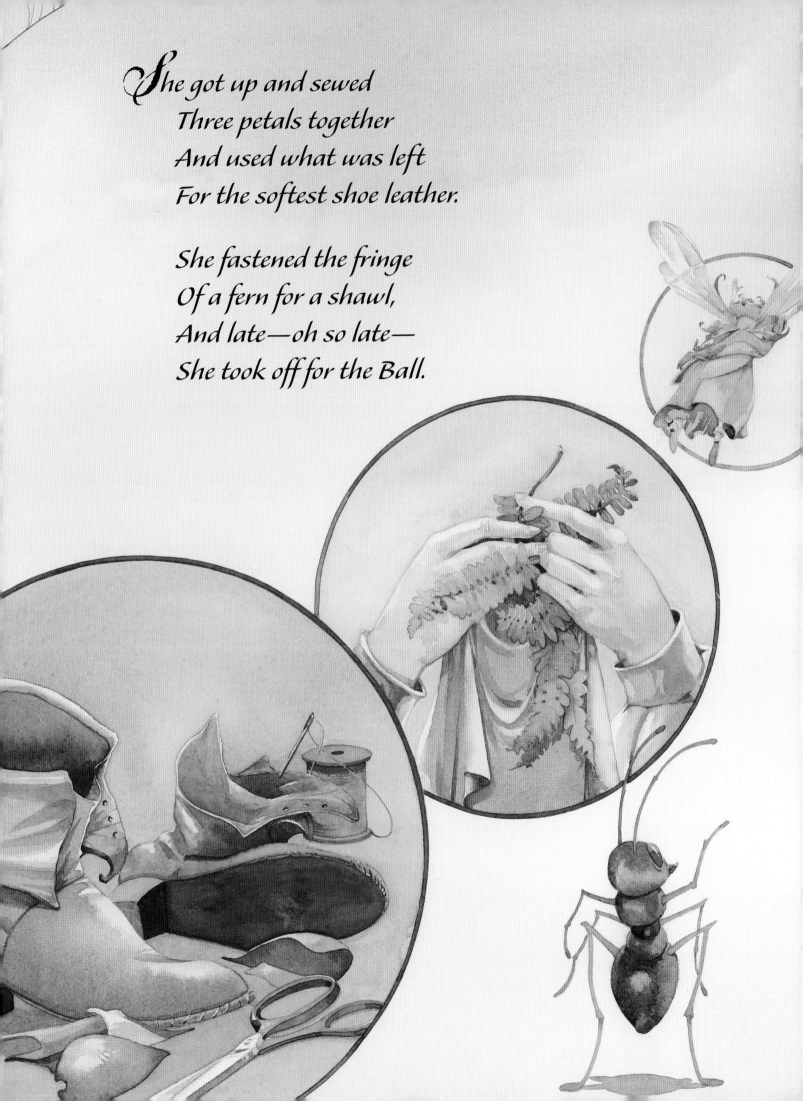

At the Hall what a clamor,
A hue and a cry.
What a fairy-folk glamour
Beset ear and eye.

There were fiddlers and fifers
And pipers and all
Who were greeting the guests
At the Fairies' own Ball.

Tiptoe and heel-toe,
They dipped and they danced.
They shook, shuffled, shimmied,
They bowed and they pranced.

They trotted and trembled,
  They waltzed, waddled, winged,
  They hopped and gavotted,
  They floated and flingged.

And just when the clock struck
    A quarter to one,
    And just when the King announced
    Dancing was done,

That one long-lost fairy
   Appeared at the gate.
   "Oh, please, sir," she wheezed. "Sir,
   I'm sorry I'm late."

"You're late!" roared the King,
And the dinner plates shook.
"You're late!" cried the Queen,
And she gave her The Look!

But the Prince of the Fairies
Came down from his throne.
He held out his hand
To that fairy alone.

"Before you arrived,
I hated this ball.
There was no one I wanted
To dance with at all.

"I told both my parents
I wanted to go.
But Mother said, 'Never!'
And Father said, 'No!'

"But then you arrived,"
He said right in her ear,

"And I want to start dancing
Because you are here."

In the year that soon followed
The two of them wed.
And the letters sent out
To the fairies all read . . .

Come one and come all,
Come great and come small,
Come winged and come wingless,
Bejeweled or ringless,
Come walking or riding,
Come gawking or gliding,
Come soaring or sliding.
Come all,
Come all to
our own Wedding Ball.